GODZILLA ™

GODZILLA ™

A junior novelization

By H.B. Gilmour

**Based on the screenplay written by
Dean Devlin & Roland Emmerich**

SCHOLASTIC INC.

New York   Toronto   London   Auckland   Sydney

FROM THE CREATORS OF INDEPENDENCE DAY

GODZILLA®

ISBN 0-590-68091-9

12 11 10 9 8 7 6 5 4 3 2 1   8 9/9 0 1 2 3/0

Printed in the U.S.A.   40

First Scholastic printing, June 1998

1

JUNE 1968 . . .

On a small island in the Pacific, a lizard climbed off its nest.

Leaving its eggs, the six-foot-long reptile crawled out of the jungle toward the sea.

Sensing danger, it stopped. Its yellow eyes shifted nervously.

Something was wrong.

A jet plane roared overhead.

A bomb shrieked to earth, exploding on impact.

The sky went white.

Then everything turned dark.

Out of a gigantic mushroom-shaped cloud, flakes of nuclear ash fell onto what was left of the island.

Thick gray dust covered the nest the lizard had tried to protect.

Only one egg remained.

Into its cracked shell seeped the deadly fumes the French nuclear bomb test had unleashed.

MORE THAN TWENTY YEARS LATER...

The big Japanese ship was full of fish and ready to return home.

Suddenly its sonar screen showed something enormous heading right for it.

Alarms blared.

"What is going on?" the ship's cook shouted from the galley.

A moment earlier, he had been preparing soup for the crew. He had been humming an old Japanese sailor's song about "Gojira," a fierce dragon that lurked beneath the waves.

Now seamen rushed past him. Alarm horns sounded.

Before anyone could answer the old cook, the ship was rocked by a tremendous thud. Something slammed into its side.

The men in the passageway fell against the steel walls and slick decks.

The cook tried to hang onto the galley door, but a second blow rocked the ship, throwing him to the floor.

A gush of seawater washed into the galley.

The frightened old man scrambled to his feet and dived into the hallway.

No sooner had he landed, when an earsplitting noise erupted.

Before him, the wall of the ship crumpled.

A huge claw tore through the steel hull.

"Gojira!" the old cook screamed.

The next evening, the old cook rocked back and forth in a hospital bed on the tiny South Pacific island of Tahiti.

A group of strangers rushed into his room. Ordering

2

the doctors and nurses out, they set up their video cameras.

A man called Phillipe, whose short dark beard was flecked with gray, hurried to the cook's bedside.

Snapping his fingers at his concerned-looking colleague, Phillipe said in French, "Jean-Claude, ask him what happened."

In rapid Japanese, the young man questioned the patient.

The old cook did not respond.

"It is no use, Phillipe." Jean-Claude shrugged. "Whatever happened to him on that ship put him in a state of shock."

"He is the only survivor," Phillipe said, taking a silver lighter out of his pocket. He flicked it on and waved the flame in front of the cook's eyes.

Slowly, the small dark eyes flickered to life.

"What did you see, old man?" Phillipe murmured, bringing the blue light closer to the cook's face.

The ancient seaman shivered suddenly.

"Gojira!" he shouted. "GOJIRA!"

2

Dr. Niko Tatopoulos, "Nick" to his friends, peered through his rain-splattered windshield at the sign.

DANGER! NUCLEAR RADIATION, it read in Russian.

Singing along to music blaring through his headphones, Nick pulled off the road.

In the shadow of the deserted Chernobyl power plant, he hopped out of his van, opened the rear doors, and removed three metal suitcases.

It was raining hard. Nick set down the metal cases, snapping open one filled with scientific equipment.

Brushing his wet hair out of his eyes, Nick pulled from his case two long cables with large spikes attached to the ends.

Wading into a muddy field, he shoved the spikes into the rain-soaked earth.

A moment later, dozens of worms began crawling out of the black ooze.

They were huge.

Nick's job was to check the results of radioactivity on Chernobyl earthworms.

Some people would call that boring, Nick guessed. Or crazy.

But for him it was a chance to study and possibly do something about the effects of nuclear fallout on living creatures.

He filled a large jar with the oversized crawlers. He sang as he worked.

He didn't hear the Russian military helicopter behind him. So he was surprised when several Russian officers rushed at him.

Scrambling to his feet, Nick tried to remember the right Russian words. "Good day, I am . . . er, here with permission —"

The Russians hurried past.

"Dr. Niko Topopolosis?" an American voice shouted over the helicopter's noise.

"It's Tatopoulos," Nick corrected the man coming toward him.

"The worm guy, right?" the man said. "I'm with the U.S. State Department."

Deftly packing up Nick's equipment, the Russian soldiers carried it back to the chopper.

"Hey," Nick called. "Where are you going? What are they doing?"

"You've just been reassigned," the tall American replied.

A FISHING VILLAGE IN PANAMA

It was not raining in Panama. Sunshine glistened off every wave in the harbor.

"Dr. Niko Topalis?" Colonel Alex Hicks offered Nick a thin smile.

5

"It's Tatopoulos," Nick corrected the colonel.

Hicks led Nick off the dock and onto a dirt road.

"Would you mind telling me what I'm doing here?" Nick asked, wringing out the wrist of his still-damp sweatshirt.

Hicks moved swiftly. "You wouldn't believe me, Tatooplus," he said, leading Nick into a clearing in the jungle.

It took Nick a minute to realize he was looking at a shattered fishing village.

"What happened here?" Nick asked, staring at splintered houses, crushed tin roofs, and torn fishing nets. Soldiers combed the ruins. Nick heard the clicking of a Geiger counter nearby. "Was it a radiation spill?" he asked.

"Something like that." Hicks stepped around a tin roof that lay on the ground, dented, as if a giant fist had karate-chopped it.

"I work for the Nuclear Regulatory Commission, but accidents and spills are not my field." Nick followed Hicks past armed guards, down a shallow slope in the jungle floor. "Do you know that you just interrupted a three-year study of the Chernobyl earthworm?"

"Sure," Hicks said. "You're the worm guy."

"The worm guy?" Nick said, annoyed. "Did you know that radioactive contamination in that area has mutated the earthworm's DNA? Do you have any idea what that means?"

"No," Hicks replied, stepping over a rotting fish, "but I have a feeling I'm about to find out."

"It means" — Nick rushed to keep up with the colonel — "that due to a man-made accident at a Russian nuclear plant, Chernobyl earthworms are now seventeen percent larger than they were before!"

"That's big," Hicks said, but he didn't seem impressed.

"Big? They're enormous!" Nick insisted. "That's what I've been trying to tell you. I'm a biologist. I study the effect of radiation on organisms. I take radioactive samples and study them."

"Okay." Hicks pointed to the ground. "Here's your sample. Study it," he said, and walked away.

"What sample?" Nick looked down. All he saw, besides his own muddy high-tops, was crushed and flattened earth. A few fish lay splattered on the ground. "I don't see it!" he shouted.

Two men were measuring the sides of the sunken area. Others swept the crater with loudly clicking Geiger counters.

Nick turned slowly.

He was standing in a shallow pit, a hollow in the jungle floor that looked like a giant footprint.

Ahead, through an area of fallen trees, he noticed another crater. In that one, too, clicking Geiger counters registered a high amount of radiation.

Climbing out of the crater, Nick saw similar holes stamped into the earth.

"It can't be," he murmured. "It's not possible."

He ran and caught up with Colonel Hicks.

"That was a footprint," Nick shouted. "I was standing *inside* a footprint!"

"That's right," Hicks agreed, heading for the command tent.

"But there's no animal in the world that can make

footprints like that," Nick said to Colonel Hicks. "Is there?"

The footprints, if that was what they truly were, had been made recently. A day or so ago at most.

"Those *are* footprints, right?" Nick asked again. "Did anyone see what made them?"

"It happened too fast," Hicks said. "No one knew what hit them."

A Jeep raced into the village.

"I've got it. The tape's in." A pudgy man waved a canvas bag stamped TOP SECRET. He scrambled out of the Jeep. "The French finally released it!"

Everyone rushed into the command tent to see the videotape.

"A Japanese cannery ship was attacked and sunk yesterday," Hicks explained to Nick as they hurried to the TV monitor. "It was near the French Polynesians."

Nick turned to the monitor.

On a white hospital bed, a shrunken old man was rocking back and forth, repeating the same word over and over.

It sounded like *Go-jeed-ah*.

"Gojira," the old man chanted. "Gojira . . . Gojira!"

3

This was her lucky day, Audrey Timmonds decided. Something *big* was going to happen. She just knew it.

Arms full of grocery bags, Audrey dashed out of the rain into the revolving doors of the WIDF TV studios.

Today she was going to be promoted from Charles Caiman's assistant to on-camera news reporter.

If her boss kept his promise.

Which he never did, Audrey reminded herself, taking the elevator to the twelfth floor newsroom.

Charles Caiman, WIDF's nightly news anchor, was not impressive-looking in person. He was kind of squat and sleazy. "Height-impaired," Audrey's best friend Lucy called him. "A legend in his own mind."

Studying his script, Caiman strutted past Audrey and Lucy, heading for the studio at the back of the office.

"Luce, should I ask him?" Audrey whispered. Remembering that it was her lucky day, she bolted after the newsman.

Caiman saw her and started walking faster.

"Mr. Caiman." She caught up with him. "Did you talk with Mr. Humphries? You promised you'd tell him how

9

well I'm doing. How I research all your best stories and write your scripts —"

"*Assist* me in writing my scripts," Caiman corrected her.

She didn't argue. Leaning against the wall was a big cardboard cutout of the WIDF news team, with a smiling Charles Caiman standing front and center.

The life-sized poster wobbled as Audrey brushed by it. "But you told him, right?" she said, steadying the shaky cutout. "You told him that I'm ready —"

But Caiman wasn't ready.

Audrey cleared her throat and tried again. "Mr. Caiman," she said, "I've been doing extra research for you after-hours and weekends for over three years —"

"I'd love to stay and chat," Caiman interrupted her, "but it's time for the grown-ups to go to work. Now, if you'll excuse me?" he said sarcastically, pushing past her and into the studio.

Through the glass, Audrey watched him size up his new co-anchor, who was about six inches taller than he.

"Box!" he hollered. A stagehand rushed over and set an apple crate down next to the newsman. Audrey watched Caiman climb up onto it.

He was the same height as his co-anchor now. A satisfied smile slid across his face.

Turning away in disgust, Audrey came face-to-face with the cardboard cutout. Taking out her gum, she stuck it on the newsman's nose.

The next day, Nick was taken to another location, Great Pedro Bluff on the Caribbean island of Jamaica.

Here, a huge cargo ship lay on its side in the sand. Gigantic holes were torn into its hull.

Three strangers were taking measurements of the jagged tears.

"Who are those guys?" Colonel Hicks demanded. "Lieutenant, get them away from there."

"They are with me," a man with a thick French accent declared. "Phillipe Roache, Colonel. La Rochelle Property and Casualty Insurance." He handed Hicks a business card. "I am the agent in charge. We are preparing a report."

At the water's edge, Nick noticed a torn crate of tuna fish. Several cans were scattered in the sand.

The clicking of a Geiger counter caught Nick's attention. He hurried back to the beached ship and examined the gashes in its side.

Something was stuck to the largest tear, something that looked like raw steak. With a pair of tweezers from his knapsack, Nick removed a piece and examined it more closely.

It was flesh, a meaty chunk of what looked like reptile flesh.

An hour later, Nick was airborne again.

Sitting on the floor of the military transport plane that had carried the research team to Jamaica, Nick was studying the specimen he'd taken from the ship. It was from the creature who'd attacked the ship. And it was radioactive.

Nick had a theory about the creature. He announced, "I believe this is a mutated aberration, a hybrid caused by the fallout in that region."

"Say what?" Colonel Hicks said.

"Worm Man thinks we're looking at a mutant monster

enjoying a nuclear growth spurt," a scientist said sarcastically.

"Like your giant earthworms?" Hicks asked.

"Yes," Nick replied excitedly. "We're seeing a never-before-known creature. The dawn of a new species. The first of its kind."

4

The old bum carried a beat-up fishing rod.

Shuffling past the smelly stalls of New York's Fulton Fish Market, he stopped to rest under the FDR Drive.

The rain would not let up. After a moment, the old bum pulled up his greasy collar, left the shelter of the overpass, and scurried out onto the pier.

At the edge of the dock, he cast his line into the murky waters.

Within seconds, the lure bobbed, and the pole bent.

Then the water started churning.

Something enormous began to lift out of the scummy river.

The huge back fins of a tremendous reptile burst from the water.

Dropping his pole, the old bum took off running. The dock behind him ripped apart as an awesome force lifted from beneath it.

The creature rose, sending a huge wave crashing down across the elevated highway, bending the steel girder like a paper clip.

A van washed over the guardrail. A yellow cab landed on top of it, crushing its hood.

Overhead, on the Drive, cars and trucks crashed and scraped against one another. Horns began to blare. People shrieked.

An enormous foot with massive claws stepped over the highway, shattering the pavement.

In one motion, a huge tail dragged across the Drive, sweeping the roadway clear of wreckage.

The earth shook as the creature moved inland toward the fish market.

A cargo truck was lifted into the air. Crushed ice and tons of fish rained down onto the street.

Sixty blocks away, midtown was awash with rain.

Soaked, Audrey ducked into the Athens Diner. "Tuna on rye," she called, sliding into the booth with Lucy and her husband, Victor "Animal" Palotti, WIDF's fearless news cameraman.

The Athens was bustling and noisy, its windows pleasantly fogged with steam. Above the counter, a television was tuned to WIDF's *News at Noon*. At least Caiman wasn't on, Audrey noted gratefully.

Across the table, Victor was digging into a cheeseburger and fries. A smear of ketchup clung to the cuff of his sweater. There was even a crumb dangling from his backwards baseball cap.

It was easy to see why everyone called him Animal, Audrey thought, smiling fondly at her best friend's husband.

"Hey, how's it goin'?" Animal mumbled, flashing her a burger-filled grin.

"My life reeks," Audrey replied.

"Oh, please," Lucy said. "*His* life reeks. How can you eat like that?" she asked her husband.

"I can't believe Caiman was such a jerk." Audrey took off her wet beret. It had looked great this morning. Now it resembled roadkill.

"You're too nice," Lucy said to Audrey, "that's your problem. You've got to be a killer to get ahead."

"Nice guys finish last," Animal added. "First rule of the jungle."

"I can be tough if I want to," Audrey insisted.

Animal gave a barking laugh that sent a burst of french fries across the table.

"Oh my gosh!" Audrey shouted as the waitress delivered her sandwich.

"'Gosh'?" Lucy shook her head. "You see what I mean? Who says 'gosh'? Gosh is so *nice*."

"No, look!" Audrey pointed to the television set. "Turn it up. Turn that up," she said, hurrying over to the TV.

The bottom of the screen read *Panama*. And there, walking alongside some military man on a pier, his raggedy knapsack strapped to his wide shoulders, his dark hair flopping over his eyes, was Nick.

"That's my college sweetie!" Audrey hollered. "Look at him. He looks so handsome on TV. What's he doing in Panama?"

A short while later, when they were up at the cashier paying for their lunch, Lucy asked, "Did your college sweetie have a name?"

"Niko Tatopoulos," Audrey told her.

"Is that why you dumped him?" Animal teased.

"Very funny," Audrey replied. "No. I couldn't picture

15

myself with someone who'd spend his summer picking apart cockroaches. It just seemed too boring."

Lucy laughed. "And now you live the glamorous life of Charles Caiman's assistant."

There was a dull thumping noise in the distance, as though an immense truck had hit a speed bump blocks away.

Audrey felt the floor of the diner shudder, very faintly, beneath her feet.

She glanced out the steamy window. All she could see through the driving rain was the camera pole of the WIDF news van parked outside.

"How long were you and this guy going steady?" Animal asked, taking a toothpick from the dispenser on the counter.

"Nearly four years," Audrey confessed.

"Girl, I'm surprised he didn't ask you to marry him," Lucy said.

"That's the problem," Audrey explained. "He did."

Suddenly the distant thumping grew louder. This time, everyone in the diner seemed to notice it.

"Tell me that's not another lame parade," Lucy said.

The next thump rattled the dishes on the counter. Glasses tumbled from a shelf behind the cashier. The toothpick dispenser fell to the floor.

"I don't think it's a parade," Animal said, whirling toward the window as another thump shook the entire building. Outside, people had begun to race through the rain.

An enormous dark shadow moved past the misty windows.

There was a screech of brakes outside, and then the unmistakable crunch of a car crash.

"Duck!" Animal yelled as a newspaper vending machine sailed directly into the front window, shattering it.

Then, suddenly, the diner was still.

"What was that?" Audrey whispered, gripping Lucy's arm. For once her friend was speechless.

"You don't want to know!" Animal assured her. "Get under the table! I've got to get this on tape."

"Victor, don't be stupid!" Lucy hollered. But he was out the door.

Water shot up from broken fire hydrants. Building wreckage fell. Cars were burning. The roof of Animal's news van had been crushed.

Dodging falling debris, Animal ran to his truck and pried open the back door.

By the time Lucy and Audrey got outside, he had grabbed his equipment and taken off running.

"No!" Lucy screamed. "Come back here, Victor, you creep!"

Trying to jam a cassette into his video camera, Animal raced around the corner.

The air was filled with smoke and steam. Cars were burning, people screaming and scattering. A greenish-brown tower Animal had never noticed before stood in the middle of the street.

Animal's jaw dropped as he scanned up the length of the tower.

It was . . . shaped like an enormous lizard. Its immense body was crusted with scales, its massive head ridged with spikes. This lizard on steroids was solid, muscular, and pulsing with life.

Just then, the mammoth creature craned its thick neck. A fold of dense skin hung from its throat. Lifting its gigantic jaw, it bellowed into the sky.

The screaming in the streets grew frantic. Windows rattled. A huge pane of department store glass shattered, crashing inches from Animal's back.

Though his heart was pounding and his hands had begun to shake, Animal forced the tape into his video camera.

Hoisting the camera onto his shoulder, he darted into the middle of the street and began videotaping the wailing beast.

The camera moved slowly and deliberately upward, taking in every detail of the terrifying lizard until it reached the creature's howling head.

That head swung down suddenly. Yellow eyes bored into Animal through the camera lens. Then the lens went black.

Animal looked out from behind the camera and saw the underside of an immense foot poised above his head, ready to squash him like a bug.

Still shooting, the cameraman raced backwards.

The foot descended recklessly.

Animal could not outrun it.

Holding the camera over his head, one finger locked on the power button, he froze beneath the falling claw, paralyzed with fear.

The creature's foot slammed down.

The ground beneath Animal shook. Amazingly, he was

not crushed. Not that he knew of, anyway. And he could see light, a sliver of light, above him.

Breathing hard, his chest heaving, Animal realized he was standing *between the lizard's toes*!

The gargantuan foot lifted abruptly.

The street rumbled again as the terrifying giant continued his mystifying march.

Animal stared in amazement as an immense tail swept past and the huge lizard disappeared around a corner.

Standing, shaking, soaked, Animal checked his camera. The red light, the shooting light, was still on.

"I got it?" Animal murmured, amazed. "I got it!" he yelled, grateful and terrified.

5

The convoy sped along the New Jersey Turnpike, then pulled into a military base still in the process of being built. On the outskirts of a small city, the base offered an awesome view of Manhattan.

Nick stared thoughtfully at the endangered island as his Jeep stopped in front of a huge command tent where a mob of reporters waited.

"We've got nothing to say right now." Sheltering the scientist from cameras and microphones, Colonel Hicks plowed through the press and into the tent.

"Sergeant O'Neal, sir," a young officer introduced himself. "The mayor has agreed to evacuate the city. He's called out the National Guard."

Throughout the busy tent, equipment was being installed — generators, telephone lines, computers, radios, and TV monitors.

"Where is the creature?" Hicks asked, ignoring the chaos around them.

"We've lost sight of him, sir," the young sergeant said crisply.

Hicks turned on him. "You want to run that by me again, son?"

Nick noticed that the back of the command tent was open. He could see the city across the way. Military helicopters circled above it, scanning the wreckage.

"I don't understand," he said to O'Neal. "How can something that large just disappear?"

The sergeant shrugged uncomfortably. "We're not sure. We're checking the area now."

"He probably returned to the river," someone suggested.

"I don't think so. Look at those buildings." Nick gestured to the soaring skyscrapers. "That's a place where he can easily hide."

A soldier ran into the tent, his face flushed with excitement. "Channel Twelve caught it on film!" he shouted, turning on one of the newly installed TV sets.

"WIDF's exclusive tape was taken less than a half hour ago," Charles Caiman was saying as Animal's camera panned up the creature's swampy underbelly.

The lizard's enormous head appeared, the flap of pale skin dangling from its throat. The jaundiced eyes glared fiercely. The cavernous mouth roared open.

Throughout the tent, workers and military personnel stopped dead in their tracks, staring at the screen.

"Cameraman Victor Palotti barely survived this vicious attack to provide us with exclusive footage," Caiman's voice continued as the beast's immense foot came down around the cameraman.

* * *

The staff of WIDF was watching the same news story. As the video ended, Audrey hugged the cameraman. "Great stuff, Animal," she said.

"Weren't you scared?" someone yelled.

"Sure. I thought Lucy was going to kill me," Animal joked.

"He was right." Lucy punched him.

"People!" Murray, the station manager, looked around anxiously. Packing crates and cartons were everywhere. "Come on!" he urged. "We've got to move to the New Jersey station before our ten o'clock broadcast. The whole city's being evacuated."

Audrey glanced at the TV monitor. Caiman was off the air. One of WIDF's field reporters was updating the story from New Jersey.

"Military and government health officials set up a base on the New Jersey coast this afternoon," the reporter said as the camera tracked people climbing out of Jeeps and rushing past waiting reporters.

And there was Nick again! Running a hand through his thick dark hair, with that big backpack slung over his shoulders, he was following this fierce guy in full uniform who kept waving the cameras away.

Looking adorable and amazingly important, Nick Tatopoulos was hurrying into a tent on the command post in New Jersey.

"Audrey!" She whirled at the sound of Caiman's voice. He was racing toward the elevator. "My bag?" He snapped his fingers at her.

Grabbing his briefcase, Audrey rushed through the office. "Mr. Caiman, I've got a lead," she said. "I know a guy on the inside with the military."

"Not now." He kept walking.

"You don't understand." She trotted alongside him. "I can get us some great background information —"

"No, *you* don't understand, honey." Caiman caught the elevator door as it was about to close. "This is when the big boys go to work." He stepped onto the elevator and pointed at her hand. "My bag?"

Snatching Caiman's ID press pass tag off his briefcase, Audrey threw the leather bag at him.

For a moment, Audrey stared at the press pass in her hand. She couldn't believe she'd stolen Caiman's ID. Then Lucy hollered, "Forget him. Get what you need and let's go!"

Outside, three million New Yorkers were trying to leave the city at once. The streets were filled with desperate people darting around stalled cars, spewing hydrants, and smoking wreckage.

Panicked pedestrians were trying to funnel into subway entrances. Audrey and Lucy joined them. In a mob of shouting, shoving commuters, they descended the subway stairs.

Minutes later, smashed together like sardines inside a subway car, Audrey watched as Lucy tried to paste her picture over Caiman's on the boss's press pass. Audrey felt uncomfortable about it.

"I don't know if this is a very good idea, Luce," she said.

"What are you talking about?" Lucy responded. "Finally you got a little chutzpah. Don't wimp out on me. How often do you think you're going to have an ex-boyfriend on the inside of a major story? This is a once-in-a-lifetime opportunity."

Reluctantly, Audrey agreed. And when Lucy finished the job, Audrey's "new" press pass looked pretty real.

Racing to his helicopter, the mayor of New York turned and waved to the crowd of anxious businesspeople he had just reassured. Unbeknownst to him, one of the people in the crowd had secretly attached a tiny microphone under his collar. Now, someone far away could eavesdrop on everything the mayor said.

In the WIDF news helicopter, Charles Caiman pulled off his mike and hollered to Animal, "Over there, that's the mayor's helicopter."

"I thought the captain was supposed to go down with the ship," Animal said, filming the silver craft with the Big Apple emblem.

"Must be going to the briefing." They were banking toward the Jersey shore. "That's it over there." Caiman pointed at the acres of tents and trucks below them.

Minutes later, Animal and Caiman were at the base. Pushing through a gawking crowd, they ran through the rain to the media area. Two police officers stopped them.

"You need press ID past this point," one of the cops said.

"Don't you watch TV?" Caiman demanded.

The police exchanged looks. "Can we see your press pass, sir?" the second officer asked mildly.

Caiman reached automatically for the pass attached to his briefcase. It was missing. "I had one here on my bag," he told the cops, flustered. The anchorman searched his pockets, growing more agitated.

Finally, Animal showed his own ID to the officers. "He's with me," the cameraman assured the police, and together they plowed through the checkpoint.

6

"The mayor is speaking now," Jean-Claude told his boss, Phillipe. "He is in the command tent. He did not detect the device that you attached to his collar. Now he is our microphone." Phillipe and his men were in a van filled with high-tech equipment.

Phillipe turned up the volume on a console. The mayor's voice came through perfectly.

"You lost him?! You're telling me that in an election month I've evacuated the entire city for nothing?!" they heard him rave.

"We've been monitoring the waters around the island," a new voice said.

Jean-Luc looked questioningly at Jean-Claude. "That is the admiral," he explained. "Admiral Phelps."

"As far as we can tell, it hasn't left the area," Phelps said.

"As far as you can tell?" It was the mayor again, annoyed. "Is that the best you people can come up with?"

"We think there's a strong reason to believe it may still

be in the city." The men in the van recognized the self-assured voice of Colonel Hicks.

"But you don't know for sure!" the mayor insisted.

"Mr. Mayor," Hicks continued in a tightly controlled voice. "We cannot give the all-clear until we've checked each and every building."

"Excuse me, sir," Sergeant O'Neal interrupted. "That may be more difficult than we originally projected."

"More good news?!" the mayor snorted sarcastically.

"We've run into a problem," O'Neal said softly.

"So this is the city that never sleeps." Nick peered out of the speeding Jeep at the deserted streets of Manhattan. He was in a convoy of military vehicles, racing downtown.

The convoy halted near the triangular Flatiron Building on lower Broadway.

Nick and the other scientists followed Colonel Hicks and Sergeant O'Neal all the way down the steps of the 23rd Street subway station. What they saw astounded them.

The separate tunnels through which the local and express trains normally ran had been destroyed. What remained was one gigantic cave — an enormous hole in which a gargantuan creature could hide.

Nick had been right. The creature *was* here, not out to sea.

Combat troops with flashlights were moving toward the hole.

They looked up. The building above them had been hollowed out and torn to shreds.

Godzilla! The mutant monster
had come to America!
But nobody knew it. Yet...

Dr. Nick Tatopoulos, a scientist, loved his work. He sang as he dug up earthworms in Chernobyl.

Nick was sent to a fishing village in Panama. A huge footprint had been sighted there. Nick was standing inside it!

Godzilla swam across the ocean toward New York City. He destroyed ships along the way. He ate a lot of fish.

Godzilla arrived in New York. He wasn't a nice guest. He first wrecked a fishing pier.

Then Godzilla took a "walking tour." He did not step lightly—he crushed everything in his path!

People panicked! They tried to get out of Godzilla's path.

Cameraman Victor "Animal" Palotti wanted to be the first to videotape Godzilla—even if he ended up between the monster's toes!

Fish was Godzilla's favorite food. Using tons of it, the U.S. army tried to lure the monster from his hiding place. Instead, they fed him.

Godzilla liked the fish, but he didn't like being hunted. He fled, right through a skyscraper.

Nick believed Godzilla was hiding underground in the subway. He also believed Godzilla was pregnant, and had laid eggs somewhere.

Nick was right! He found hundreds of Godzilla's eggs with Baby Godzillas about to hatch. If they did, they could take over the world. Nick had to stop them.

Uh-oh—too late! The Baby Godzillas were everywhere! In the end, Nick and his team managed to destroy them all. Or did they?

"We figure he crashed through the building from the street. Then he ripped up the floors, crawled down into the subway, and carved out his cave," Sergeant O'Neal told them. "When we learned he could burrow through the tunnels, we realized he could be out of the quarantine zone."

"How many tunnels lead off the island?" a scientist broke in.

"Five," O'Neal replied. "We've checked them all. He hasn't used any of them."

"Have them sealed off," Colonel Hicks ordered.

"And how should we do that, sir?" O'Neal asked.

"Fill them with cement, land mines, bombs," Hicks barked. "Just make sure that thing doesn't leave this island."

Nick watched the armed troops moving around inside the tunnel. "You know, he's not an enemy trying to evade you," he said. "He's just an animal."

"An animal? Did you see that thing on TV?" O'Neal shook his head. "We're not talking about some cat or dog here."

"What are you suggesting?" Hicks asked Nick.

"When I needed to catch earthworms," he explained, "I knew the best way to catch them was not to dig them out, but to *lure* them out."

"Sergeant!" a voice from the tunnel called nervously. "There's stuff flopping around in here."

"All we need to do," Nick continued, "is find out what the creature needs and he'll come to us."

"Like what?" Colonel Hicks wanted to know. "What could it need?"

"Fish," the soldier in the tunnel shouted suddenly. "Sergeant, there's fish stashed away in here. Whew. Fish everywhere."

Colonel Hicks looked at Nick. "Fish? Is that what we need to draw him out?"

"Looks like it," Nick agreed.

7

The military prepared to lure Godzilla with fish. Once the beast was out in the open, soldiers, poised on rooftops, would shoot him. Apache helicopters and mobile rockets were in place to finish the job.

No one knew it, but those plans were being overheard by the mysterious Frenchman, Phillipe, and his team. That tiny recording device secretly attached to the mayor was still working. Everything he said, or that was being said around him in the command tent, could be heard by the French team. They could also be seen, via high-tech equipment.

According to plan, a dozen huge trucks dumped tons of fish into Flatiron Square. Nick, in the center of the action, watched in amazement.

"Oh, man." Sergeant O'Neal grimaced at the smell.

"That's a lot of fish," Nick agreed as a mountain of shiny-wet tuna, salmon, and pike piled up.

When the trucks left, O'Neal headed up to the rooftop command post overlooking Flatiron Square.

Nick stayed at the sandbag barrier, where two young officers were manning communications gear. The video monitor beside them showed different aerial views of the sector.

Everything looked ready.

Nothing was happening.

Five, then eight minutes passed.

Nick scanned the square. The stillness was spooky. Something was wrong.

"No!" Nick's voice broke the silence.

Sprinting into the street, he rushed toward a manhole cover inches from the mountain of fish.

Falling to his knees, Nick tried to remove the heavy steel cover.

"What's up?" O'Neal radioed from the rooftop.

"We've got to open the manholes!" Nick hollered. "The scent of the fish has to get down to him."

O'Neal gave the order, and Nick stepped back as soldiers rushed into the street to dislodge the heavy disks.

They were almost finished when he spotted a manhole cover in place down a side street.

Nick raced out of the square to the intersection and tried to wrestle the steel hatch out of the gutter.

Kneeling in the street, he heard a noise. It came up through the manhole, from underground. A vibrating rumble, like the distant thunder of a low-flying jet, Nick thought.

Half a block away, two parked cars jolted suddenly, banging against each other.

The gutter beneath them buckled.

A crack split the pavement, traveling quickly along the street, directly toward the manhole.

Nick scrambled to his feet, backing away from the hole.

With a deafening roar, the ground erupted.

The mammoth beast burst through, ripping up the street as he rose.

Nick watched, awestruck, as the immense reptile broke free of the pavement and, with a roar that sent wreckage clanging through the street, pulled himself upright.

He was taller than the buildings around him.

His huge head with its spiked crown craned up at the night sky.

His chest, roped with muscles, heaved as he sniffed the air.

With its ridge of huge scales, the mutant's tail seemed to go on for blocks.

Nick pulled a disposable camera from his pocket and snapped a picture.

The flashbulb's glare alerted the beast. His colossal head swooped down close to Nick's.

Suddenly the street was filled with soldiers. Guns trained, rocket launchers shouldered, they surrounded the giant lizard.

But the sight of him paralyzed them. They stared up, frozen in amazement.

Nick signaled gently for them not to fire.

Sensing that the danger had passed, the beast lifted its fearsome head, stepped over Nick, and moved toward the square.

On the roof of the Flatiron Building, O'Neal and his men gazed in shock as the enormous creature walked past them to the fish.

They watched, riveted, until his monstrous tail whipped by, smashing two of the cameras as the startled soldiers dived for cover.

While the mutant feasted on the fish, the troops gaped, weapons idle in their hands.

Miles across the river, Colonel Hicks and his staff watched the monitors, astonished. Everyone in the tent stood stunned before the screen.

Finally, Hicks grabbed the radio. "Fire at will!" he ordered.

O'Neal delivered the message to his troops. "Fire! Now!"

The soldiers snapped out of their stupor. "No! Wait," Nick shouted. But his words were lost in a firestorm of bullets.

The humongous creature reared up, screaming.

His immense tail swept a dozen armed men from the street, tossing them against walls and windows with devastating force.

Three sidewinder missiles flew from the launcher in the park. Their screeching whine alerted the beast. He ducked, and the missiles slammed into the building behind him, exploding on impact.

Bricks and glass rained down. Video cameras blew up as they hit the street.

Nick ran for cover. As he raced across Broadway, a bronze statue toppled off its pedestal, trapping him, unharmed, beneath it.

Nick couldn't escape, but he could roll onto his back. He saw an armored battalion moving against the creature. "Watch out!" he shouted.

Spinning, the mutant lizard bulldozed through the tanks. Mashing several underfoot, he raced out of the square.

In New Jersey, Colonel Hicks stared at a bank of monitors that showed only static or devastation. "O'Neal," Hicks radioed, "what's going on?!"

"He's gone. Heading north, sir," the sergeant responded.

Hicks turned to his map table. "Get me Echo division. They should be in Times Square with six armored vehicles."

A soldier handed Hicks the radio. "Echo division, any sight of him?" he asked.

"He's kind of hard to miss, sir," a shaky voice responded. "We've only got four AVs left. They're chasing him, but he's fast."

"Fire at him," Hicks snapped. "That'll slow him down."

"Hasn't so far," the officer reported. "He creamed two of our tanks. Oh, no!" the soldier yelped. "He just stubbed his toe on another one. Flipped it over."

"Order in an air strike. Now!" Hicks shouted to his aides.

Moments later, the combat helicopters swooped down. "He's moving fast, but we've got him locked on," the lead pilot radioed.

The choppers came screaming down, firing rockets.

The creature wheeled abruptly, disappearing around a corner.

The rockets blasted into the Chrysler Building. Shards of glass exploded as the landmark structure crumbled.

"Did you get him?" Hicks shouted.

"That is a negative impact," the pilot reported.

"Negative impact!?!" It was the mayor. "It's the Chrysler Building," he screeched. "Your people are destroying my city!"

"I thought you said he was locked on!" Hicks demanded.

"Sir," the pilot responded, zooming around the corner in pursuit, "the heat seekers can't lock. He's colder than the buildings around him."

All four helicopters slowed and carefully scanned the street.

The lead pilot spotted an enormous hole torn into an old factory. He pointed down at it.

Nodding, the others opened fire, destroying what was left of the building.

A scream of pain echoed through the narrow street. It seemed to come from the smoldering remains of the bombed factory.

The Apache pilots stopped firing and stared into the smoking wreckage. "I think we got him," one of them said.

He was wrong.

With a bloodcurdling roar, the monster exploded from a building behind them.

His fierce breath twisted the blades of the nearest chopper. It crashed into a building, then plunged to earth.

The colossal jaws snapped shut on two others, crushing them.

With a swipe of his deadly claw, the beast swatted the last Apache out of the sky.

Sergeant O'Neal and several of his men lifted the statue off Nick.

The square was a disaster. The rubble of the missile attack lay scattered among the few fish the creature had left behind.

"You all right?" Sergeant O'Neal asked.

"I'm fine," Nick answered. Then he knelt down and saw something on the ground — reddish-brown liquid. Instantly, Nick realized what it was: Godzilla's blood. He took out a small glass container and scooped up a sample.

"I can't believe it," O'Neal was saying. "He did all this, and basically we did nothing to him."

"That's not true," Nick noted. "We fed him."

8

Audrey had pasted her own picture over Caiman's. Wearing the fake press pass, she pushed through the crowd gathered at the gates of the military base.

A line of trucks and Jeeps was approaching, and suddenly everyone rushed toward it.

Swarming news crews blocked the convoy's path, forcing it to stop.

In the fourth car back, Nick peered out at the mobbed street and noticed a pharmacy. Clutching the blood sample he'd gotten from the creature, he hurried into the drugstore. Nick had a hunch and needed something at the drugstore to see if he was right.

He was paying for his purchases when a voice behind him said, "Nick?!"

Nick turned.

"Audrey?!" he said, instantly grinning. "Is it really you?"

She was smiling, too. "It's good to see you, Nick," she said. He scooped up his change and they walked out together.

"So, you made it." He pointed at Caiman's press card. "You're a reporter."

Audrey changed the subject. "You still picking apart cockroaches?"

"I'm into earthworms now." Nick's grin faded. "But I don't want to *bore* you with my work."

"You're still mad at me?" she said. "That was years ago, Nick."

"You left me without a phone call, a letter, nothing," he replied. "I guess I am a little mad." To his surprise, Audrey looked hurt. "But you're right," he said. "It's been a long time. Can I offer you a cup of tea?"

The small private tent in which Nick's minilab was set up reminded Audrey of his messy book-filled college room, where they'd laughed and argued and studied together.

"So exactly what are you doing with worms?" she asked as Nick ripped open the drugstore packages and began mixing the contents together.

"I'm working for the Nuclear Regulatory Commission," he said, snapping open his metal equipment case.

He took a beaker from the case. "I'm doing a study for the government on new species that have been created as a direct result of nuclear contamination," Nick explained, pouring his mixture into the beaker.

"Nuclear contamination?" Audrey was suddenly alert. "Is that what you think caused this creature? What else do you know about it?"

Nick added the blood sample to his mixture. Then he took a piece of paper from one of the drugstore boxes and dipped it into the mix.

"Well, we know he eats tons of fish," Nick replied, glancing at his watch. "And that he's of the reptile genus. Obviously, he's a burrower. He's amphibious, and —" He pulled out the paper and examined it. "And . . . he's pregnant!"

"*He* is?" Audrey said, confused.

Excited, Nick began to gather his materials together. "I just bought a bunch of home pregnancy tests. Obviously they weren't designed for this. But basically they look for the same patterns —"

"I don't get it," Audrey interrupted. "If it's a new species, the first of its kind, how can it be pregnant? Doesn't it need a mate?"

"Not necessarily. Many organisms reproduce without mating." Nick began to pace excitedly. "I kept wondering why he would travel all this way. But it makes perfect sense. All kinds of creatures have been known to go great distances for reproduction. That's why he came to New York. He's nesting!"

"Nesting?" Audrey echoed.

"Do you realize that a lizard can lay as many as a dozen eggs at a time?" Gathering up the beaker and his blood sample, Nick moved to the door of the tent. "Audrey, I'm sorry, but I've got to get this into the lab right away. I'll be back as soon as I can, okay?"

"Sure," she said. "Go on."

Nick rushed out. Audrey waited for a while.

She noticed a television set in the corner. Audrey walked over to it and saw a videotape sitting on the VCR. Curious, she popped the cassette into the machine and turned on the TV.

What she saw was a wrinkled old Japanese man rocking back and forth on a hospital bed. Someone was asking him questions. But the man kept repeating only one word, "Gojira," over and over.

Audrey hit fast-forward. The tape whirred ahead to a view of enormous footprints tracking through a jungle. She fast-forwarded again and saw a ship stranded on a beach. Its side had been torn as if huge claws had ripped through its hull.

Audrey's heart began to pound. Had she stumbled onto a video that showed the damage the mutant lizard had done?

What a story, what an exclusive!

She rewound the tape and stared at the blank screen, torn about what to do. It was Nick's cassette. She could wait until he came back and . . . what? Ask him for it? Tell him that she was desperate to become what he already thought she was, a real reporter?

You've got to be a killer to get ahead, she heard Lucy urging. *Nice guys finish last,* Animal had advised.

Audrey popped out the tape and stuck it into her purse.

Rain began to drum on the roof of the tent. She peeked outside.

The WIDF news van was parked outside the compound gates.

Audrey dashed through the downpour, hoping that the computers in the truck were hooked up. She had some research to do. And she had to find Animal.

He was inside the van, shooting the breeze with Ed Mullins, one of the editors.

"Great!" Audrey cried, shaking the rain out of her hair. "I've got some major footage for a segment I want you to shoot and edit. But first, I've got to write the piece."

"Sure," Mullins said. "Who's going to report it?"

"I am," she announced, rushing to the computer.

It was morning when they finished taping. Locked in the editing bay, they watched Audrey's story.

"From an old Japanese sailor's song called '*Gojira*,'" her voice came through the speakers, "a mythological sea dragon who attacked sailors, to our own modern-day terror. . . ."

"It's a real good piece, Audrey," Animal said as Ed rewound the tape. "How'd you get the material?"

She thought of Nick and winced. "From . . . a friend."

The command tent was filled with military and government brass when Nick entered.

Colonel Hicks stood before a map of Manhattan. "If we lure him into a more open area, such as this portion of Central Park," he said, tapping the map, "we should be able to take him down."

"Take him down?" the mayor shouted. "Last time you didn't even scratch him!"

"That's not true," Hicks said angrily. "Our worm guy — er, I mean, Dr. Tatopoulos — found blood."

"Yes, I did," Nick said as all eyes turned to him. "And that blood indicates that the creature is about to lay eggs. Or already has."

"Are you saying there's *another* one of those things out there?" the governor asked as Hicks's jaw dropped.

"No," Nick replied, "but if we don't find the nest, *dozens* more will be born, each one capable of laying eggs."

"All right, then." Colonel Hicks called for quiet. "First we'll kill it, then we'll search for the nest."

"It may be too late by then," Nick said. "The eggs could hatch very quickly. He's not gathering fish for himself, sir. He's preparing to feed his young."

Suddenly everyone was speaking at once. "If Dr. Tatopoulos is right," O'Neal said, "we've got to act quickly."

"On some wild theory?" Hicks objected. "I say blast him. We don't have men to spare for an egg hunt!"

An aide entered the tent and whispered something to the governor. "Gentlemen, there's something I think we'd better see," the governor announced as his aide turned on a TV set.

There was the Japanese cook, rocking on his hospital bed. The image of the terrified old man froze, and Charles Caiman's face replaced it.

"From an old Japanese sailor's song called '*Godzilla*,'" Caiman announced, "a mythological sea dragon who attacked sailors, to our own modern-day terror. Who is this Godzilla, where did he come from, and why is he here? Tune in to my special report tonight. . . ."

Across the street from the base, where Audrey and Animal were eating lunch, the television was also tuned to WIDF.

"It's *Gojira*, you moron!" Audrey jumped up. "And that is not *your* report. It's mine!" she yelled at the TV. "He stole my report! That's *my* story! I'm the one who found that stupid song!"

Audrey wadded up her napkin and threw it at the TV. "Caiman, you reek!" she shouted.

9

What a sneaky, rotten jerk Caiman was. And what a jerk she'd been, Audrey thought. She ran outside the diner to look for a phone booth.

She only hoped Nick had been too wrapped up in work to watch TV. If she could just get to him before he saw that dumb story.

A guy lugging suitcases was coming out of the compound. It was Nick! He was getting into a taxi, which had just pulled up outside the base.

"Newark Airport," Nick told the cabbie.

Audrey ran through the rain to him. "Why are you leaving? It's because of me, right? Because of the story?"

"What did you think was going to happen?" he said.

Animal had seen Audrey dash out of the diner. Stuffing half a doughnut into his mouth, he ran outside to find out what was up. He heard Audrey say, "I'm sorry. Nick, when we broke up and I came to New York, I was so sure I'd make it. But I haven't. I'm not a reporter. I'm a failure. That's why I needed this story so badly —"

Nick climbed into the cab. "Good luck in your new career," he said, slamming the door. "I really think you have what it takes."

"I'm sorry," Audrey said softly as the taxi drove off.

Animal took a step toward her, changed his mind, jumped into his van, and roared off after the cab — which was heading *away* from the airport.

The taxi drove to a deserted street full of warehouses.

"Hello. Excuse me." Nick tapped on the glass partition. "This isn't the way to the airport."

The driver didn't even turn his head.

"Do you speak English?" Nick asked. "I said Newark Airport. Excuse me. All right, stop the car, right now!"

To his surprise, the cab stopped. The driver turned to face him. His tightly cropped salt-and-pepper hair and craggy face seemed strangely familiar. He slid open the glass partition. "I am afraid I cannot do that," the cabbie said in heavily accented English.

"Hey, I know you, don't I?" Nick asked, eyeing him suspiciously.

"I don't think so," the driver insisted.

"Yes." Nick remembered. "You're that insurance guy."

"I am Agent Phillipe Roache," the bearded man confessed. He pulled out a badge and opened it for Nick to see. "Of the SDECE. The French Secret Service. Your American friends are not going to look for the nest."

"Are you sure?" Nick asked, alarmed. "How do you know?"

"We know," Phillipe said. "Trust me."

"Trust you! You hijacked me," Nick said. "Why would I trust you?"

"Because, Dr. Tatopoulos," the French secret agent

replied, "you are the only one who wants to find the nest as much as I do."

A few minutes later, Phillipe drove into a warehouse filled with guns, explosives, Jeeps, trucks, and even fully armored tanks.

Phillipe's men greeted Nick like old friends.

"How did you get this stuff into the country?" Nick asked, astonished at the military hardware piled up around them.

"In America," Jean-Luc replied, "there is nothing you cannot buy."

"So why all the secrecy?" Nick asked. "Why aren't you guys working with the U.S. military?"

"I love my country. It is my job to protect it," Phillipe explained. "Sometimes I must even protect it from myself, from mistakes we have made. Mistakes we do not want the world to know about."

Nick understood. "You mean the nuclear tests in the Pacific."

"Yes," Phillipe confessed. "This testing left a terrible mess."

"The radioactive fallout," Nick said.

"I believe the fallout infected some of the area's species and helped to create this situation," Phillipe said. "We are here to clean it up."

An hour later, they were studying a map of Manhattan.

Unbeknownst to them, Animal, soaked to the skin, was outside, standing on a trash bin, peeking in at them through a small, high window.

"We know how to get into the city," Phillipe was telling Nick. "We just do not know where to start looking."

"Here," Nick said. "The subway station at Twenty-third Street. With a little luck, it will lead us right to him."

By the time Animal got home, Audrey was crying in the guest room. She'd come to stay with him and Lucy when Manhattan was evacuated.

"It's all my fault," she sobbed. "What have I done? I totally messed up with the only man who ever really cared about me."

"You could make it all up to him," Animal said.

"How?" Audrey wailed.

Animal explained his plan. He'd overheard everything Phillipe told Nick. He knew they were planning to sneak back into Manhattan and find Godzilla's nest.

"And," he told Audrey, "if Nick finds it, you should be the one to show the world he was right all along."

10

"They have prepared his dinner," Jean-Claude reported as Phillipe's men raced down the steps of the 23rd Street subway station.

Jean-Claude was listening in on a conversation between Colonel Hicks and Sergeant O'Neal. "The meadow in Central Park is filled with fish. They have tanks, rockets, and soldiers ringing the area."

"If Nick is correct, Godzilla will leave the nest soon. Ready?" Phillipe turned to Nick.

"Let's do it." Hopping off the platform, Nick led the men past an old subway car, into the torn tunnel.

A dozen flashlight beams crisscrossed the floor, following a trail of dead fish. The deeper they moved into the cave, the more fish they found.

Half a mile behind them, Animal kicked open a door and burst onto the platform.

Audrey rushed after him.

They could see beams of light moving in the distance. "That's them." Animal shouldered his video camera. They jumped off the platform and raced toward the tunnel.

The ground began to quake. Dust fell from the ceiling. "Oh, no," Audrey murmured.

Half a mile ahead, Nick was kneeling, searching through his backpack for a battery, when the tremor hit.

A terrible screeching filled the tunnel.

Nick clambered to his feet. Phillipe's team stopped in their tracks. "Godzilla!" Jean-Luc screamed.

A massive claw burst through the wall.

The men dived into a huge sewer pipe, which rattled wildly as the creature crashed through the tunnel and pounded past them.

The entire station shook. At the entrance to the tunnel, Audrey and Animal raced into the old subway car and dropped to the floor.

Audrey peeked out in time to see the giant lizard climbing through the station ceiling. Godzilla was leaving his underground lair.

Inside the tunnel, Nick and the assault team emerged from the pipe. Nick stared at the hole the reptile had ripped in the wall. "I guess we go this way," he said.

"Over there." Phillipe's flashlight found the end of the tunnel.

Nick put on a burst of speed, sprinting out into an immense dark space. The men followed. Their flashlights quickly took stock of the building.

It had been torn to shreds. Scattered fish were everywhere.

"It's Penn Station!" Nick said, stunned. "Or what's left of it."

There was a gigantic hole in the tall ceiling. "What is up there?" Phillipe asked.

But Nick's flashlight was focused on a huge sign that had crashed down. MADISON SQUARE GARDEN, it read.

"It's the scoreboard," Nick murmured. "That's Madison Square Garden up there. It's New York's most famous sports arena," he explained. "This is Godzilla's nest."

Nick knew that whatever Godzilla did on the outside, he would not lead the military back to his hidden nest.

Nick was right. The giant lizard dashed into the Hudson River. Perhaps he thought he'd be safe there.

He was wrong.

For the military had an underwater surprise waiting for Godzilla. Three nuclear submarines, all poised to fire torpedoes and destroy him.

The underwater battle between Godzilla and the submarines was fierce and bloody. When it was all over, two subs were destroyed.

But finally, so was Godzilla.

Or so everyone thought.

11

Audrey and Animal moved cautiously through Penn Station.

"Oh, man, no," Animal grumbled as their flashlights found the fallen scoreboard. "That big freak wiped out the Garden, too. No more Knicks games. No more Rangers."

Audrey stared at the hole in the station's ceiling. "You think that's where his nest is?"

"I don't know," Animal said, "but something's moving around up there."

"Now what?" Audrey whispered.

Animal raised his flashlight to a cable dangling from the hole in the ceiling. "We climb," he said.

Madison Square Garden was pitch-black. Jean-Luc had found the main circuit board and was trying to get the electricity working again.

In a corner of the trashed auditorium, Phillipe's flashlight picked out a strange clump of tall objects.

"Eggs," Nick said softly.

They stared in disbelief at a pile of reptile eggs — each one nearly twice as tall as they were.

"Only three." Nick surveyed the towering clump. "I thought there'd be more."

"You were right." A few feet away, Jean-Claude was staring at dozens of eggs lit by the assault team's flashlights.

Nick whistled softly, impressed. "There must be over twenty."

At that moment, Jean-Luc threw the main switch. The trashed arena was flooded with light.

Hundreds of huge eggs were clumped inside the cavernous space!

Nick was speechless. Phillipe turned slowly, taking in the staggering sight. Then he quickly issued orders, and his men began planting explosives around the eggs.

"We do not have enough dynamite," Jean-Claude reported moments later.

Wading through heaps of fish, Phillipe hurried to Nick, who was halfway up the bleachers, studying a group of eggs.

Several yards away, behind another pile of enormous eggs, Animal and Audrey reached the arena. Before Audrey got to her feet, Animal began filming.

Phillipe didn't notice the intruders. Neither did any of his men, who were busy planting the last of the dynamite. "Nick, we have a problem," he said, climbing up the broken bleachers.

Nick's ear was pressed against the shell of an egg.

With a loud splintering noise, the egg began to crack.

Nick and Phillipe jumped back, startled. The huge egg rattled as the creature inside it awakened.

More eggs began to crack.

Below them, on the floor of the arena, work halted.

Jean-Claude scrambled to his feet. Another of Phillipe's men, Pierre, set down his bag of explosives. Jean-Luc reached for his gun.

One by one, the assault team backed slowly away from the eggs.

Hidden in the forest of tall eggs, Audrey backed away, too. Only Animal waded forward, videotaping the hatching eggs.

The egg behind Nick and Phillipe exploded.

They whirled, stunned, as a terrible, small version of the enraged lizard burst from its shell with a chilling wail.

A few feet away, another egg broke. Another spine-tingling cry announced the birth of a terrifying new beast. "The babies!" Jean-Claude shouted. "They are alive!"

Shrieks and sounds of shells breaking filled the arena. For the moment, the scaly, wet creatures busied themselves gobbling up fish.

"I think we should leave now," Phillipe said softly, backing carefully down the bleacher steps.

"Good idea," Nick agreed.

They moved as silently as possible between the rattling eggs and splattering shells, toward the exit. Phillipe took out his radio. "Everyone outside! Now!" he commanded.

A Baby Godzilla with a fish hanging from its jaw moved toward Audrey.

"Animal," Audrey hissed, "let's get out of here!"

"One more second," Animal said, still filming. "This is fantastic."

Then he saw the small, alert creature approaching. "Time to go," he said.

Another baby appeared on the other side of them.

"Be cool," Animal whispered as Audrey backed up, bumping into him. "Don't scare them."

He led her backwards, toward the hallway through which sports teams entered the playing floor. Somewhere inside it there were dressing rooms and, Animal hoped, an exit to the street.

Eggs were cracking all around them. The two babies had finished their fish and begun to sniff at Audrey.

An egg splintered next to her. A scaly arm shot out of the shell, grabbing her leg. Claws pinched her ankle. She screamed.

Animal began battering the powerful arm with his flashlight. Frantically, Audrey kicked free of the creature. They both took off running.

"Lock the doors!" Phillipe called into the radio. "We must keep them inside!" Nick tore off his belt and wrapped it around the door handles, tying them shut.

At the other end of the arena, Jean-Claude and Jean-Luc each raced toward a different exit door. Others were doing the same.

All around them, the newborns were feasting on fish.

An egg cracked as two of Phillipe's men hurried past it.

Screeching with hunger, the creature that popped out of the egg sniffed the air. Its head whirled toward the men.

"Oh, no," one whispered. "He smells us."

"He wants fish," the other assured him.

"Yes, and that is what we smell like!"

Audrey and Animal had reached the team entrance.

They raced through the passageway to the street exit. The doors were jammed.

Audrey spun around. Three babies were blocking their return to the arena. Animal was filming them!

Audrey grabbed his arm, dragged him into a locker room, and bolted the door.

Instantly, the door was jolted by thuds. The newborns were trying to break in.

Audrey leaned against a table, trying to catch her breath. "Now what do we do?"

The door shook again. One of its hinges began to come loose. Audrey threw back her head and closed her eyes. A second later, her eyes shot open. She was staring at a ceiling vent.

"Come on," she ordered Animal, who was piling benches against the door. "Help me move this table."

She climbed up and yanked out the grate covering the air vent. "Can we fit up there?" she asked.

"Only one way to find out," Animal said, lifting her toward the vent.

In one of the hallways circling the arena, Nick and Phillipe raced from door to door, doing their best to lock the raging creatures inside.

In the corridors above and below them, teams of Phillipe's men were doing the same. Several of them had encountered the babies. Not all the men had survived.

The auditorium was filled with hatched beasts fighting over fish. One of the creatures began to sniff at Nick and Phillipe.

Suddenly the baby sped up the aisle toward them.

Phillipe slammed the door. Nick smashed the glass

cover of a nearby fire hose and wrapped the hose around the door handles.

As the newborn threw itself against the door, Phillipe tossed Nick his cell phone. "Contact the military. They must bomb this building before these things escape," he hollered, racing to secure the next exit. "Dial 555-7600. Tell them it's a Code Dragonfly. That should get you through."

Amazed, Nick dialed . . . and got a busy signal. He tried the number four more times and then tried 911 and then dialed Operator. All lines were busy.

"I can't get through." Nick chased after Phillipe. The banging on the doors was increasing. Soon one of them would give.

Jean-Claude arrived with his team. Their uniforms were soaked and bloody. "We've secured the doors on the upper levels," he reported. "The other men didn't make it."

Phillipe nodded grimly. "Nick, we'll hold them here. You must get help."

Nick raced down the stairs as Phillipe's men snapped together their automatic rifles, preparing for the fight.

On the main floor, Jean-Luc and two others circled the hallway, heading for their posts. "Get the other exits. I'll guard these," he ordered.

As his men disappeared around the bend, Jean-Luc rushed to double-check the doors. He stopped dead in his tracks. One of them was broken. It hung wide open from a single hinge.

The secret agent turned slowly. As he did, a dozen screeching beasts pounced. Jean-Luc fired his automatic rifle, but he was overrun.

"Jean-Luc! What's happened?" Jean-Claude called. He was at his post, one landing above. "Jean-Luc?" Suddenly the door behind Jean-Claude collapsed. A wave of creatures flooded out into the corridor, stampeding him.

The hallways were filling with frantic beasts. Nick was racing toward the exit when a door burst open and a herd of them thundered toward him.

He skidded around a corner and saw the elevator straight ahead. Slamming the button, he yelled, "Come on, come *on*!"

The babies moved toward him from both sides. "This is so not good," Nick muttered, pumping the button.

The elevator doors opened. Nick jumped inside, frantically pressing "Close."

"These things never work!" he hollered over the cries of the hungry babies.

One of the creatures leaped forward as the doors began to shut. Its howling head got stuck in the closing doors.

Panicked, Nick kicked it. The beast fell back. The doors shut.

At the next floor, Phillipe was standing guard. He heard the elevator stop and swerved his gun around, ready to shoot.

"It's me!" Nick shouted, jumping out. He dialed the command center again. It was still busy. "The babies are all over the place," he told Phillipe. "I can't get out of the building."

There was a fierce rattling overhead. Phillipe raised his automatic. "They're in the vents," Nick murmured, panicked.

Just then the grate in the ceiling collapsed. A video

camera crashed to the floor. Animal and Audrey tumbled out.

In a flash, Phillipe had his weapon pointed at their heads. "Who are you?" he demanded.

"It's okay," Nick said. "I know her."

12

An angry mob was gathered at the Brooklyn Bridge. Television cameras scanned the crowd. Reporters stuck microphones into furious faces.

"Godzilla's dead!" a man yelled.

"It said on the radio they torpedoed him," a woman called, "so why can't we go home?"

"Why can't we go home?" Suddenly Charles Caiman's face filled the screen. "That's what millions of New Yorkers are asking now that word has leaked of the death of Godzilla, the beast that stalked New York."

At that moment back in the command tent the mayor of New York slammed down the phone and rushed to Colonel Hicks.

"Do you have any idea what's going on out there?" the mayor ranted. "The phones are ringing off the hook with people screaming to get back into Manhattan."

Hicks was at the map table, surrounded by smiling generals and admirals. "We're sending divers into the river to retrieve the body," he explained.

"That thing's dead," the mayor pressed. "What are we waiting for?"

Hicks wasn't sure. He wished Tatopoulos hadn't pulled that dumb stunt. He needed Nick's input now.

A scientist rushed over. "Colonel, we've got to begin the search for the nest," she reminded him.

"There is no nest!" It was the mayor. "Come on!" he barked, his fleshy face turning red. "Open Manhattan, Hicks. It's over."

Phillipe lowered his gun. "You are a television reporter?" he asked Animal.

Animal replied, "I'm a cameraman."

"I see." Phillipe fired at the fallen video camera, ripping the camera apart. "No pictures," he said.

"What are you doing here?" Nick asked Audrey.

"You said there'd only be a dozen eggs!" she said irritably.

Fierce thudding rattled a door, startling them.

"Do you have a radio, a walkie-talkie?" Phillipe asked, spinning toward the noise, his weapon aimed at the door. "Anything we can use to contact the outside?"

The door shuddered. They backed away from it, moving deeper into the corridor.

"How 'bout the phones?" Animal asked.

"Circuits are overloaded," Nick explained.

"I know how you can get a message out of here," Audrey said after a moment.

The door burst open. A herd of babies galloped into the hallway. "This way!" Audrey hollered. She took off running. The men followed.

Bolting door after door behind them, they trailed Audrey up damaged stairways to a room filled with television equipment.

"How'd you know about this?" Nick asked as they locked themselves inside the broadcast booth. Its huge window offered a frightening view of the horrors below, the trashed arena filled with frenzied creatures searching for food.

"Our network covers the Ranger games," Audrey reported, sliding behind a huge console. "We've got a direct feed to our computer system."

"Which means we can contact your station, but they won't be able to get through to the military any more than I did," Nick reasoned as Phillipe and Animal shoved equipment against the door.

"When you worked with the military," Animal asked Nick, "did they watch news broadcasts?" Nick nodded. "Okay, then." Animal threw his coat to the floor and started checking out the TV cameras in the booth. "We'll go live! We'll broadcast from here and pray that your pals at command central are watching."

The WIDF news truck was parked in the shadow of the Brooklyn Bridge. Inside the van, Ed Mullins was watching Caiman's newscast when the computer started beeping. He switched on the monitor.

And there was Audrey Timmonds, looking like death on toast! "If you're seeing this, Ed, please put us on live," she was saying.

No way, Ed thought.

Just then, Animal swung his camera off Audrey and pointed it out the control booth window at the rioting beasts below.

In the news truck, Ed's eyes nearly popped out of his head.

"Ed, you see that?" Audrey was saying. "They'll be all over the city if we don't stop them."

The stunned editor rushed to his console and went to work.

The mood in the command tent was festive. The generals were preparing to leave. Hicks hadn't promised anything, but the mayor was sure the stubborn colonel would open the city soon.

Sergeant O'Neal and some of his men were watching the news. They cheered as Caiman announced, "Fears have been allayed thanks to the dedicated work of our boys in uniform."

Suddenly the smug newsman's face was replaced. "Are we on?" a young woman was asking. "Are we live?"

Plaster dust matted her hair. Her clothes were in tatters. She cleared her throat and said, "I'm Audrey Timmonds of WIDF-TV. We're live from inside Madison Square Garden, where Dr. Niko Tatopoulos has discovered the beast's lair. Doctor, tell us what is happening here."

"Shhhh. Hold it." O'Neal quieted his men.

Suddenly Nick appeared on the screen, looking even worse than the reporter. "We've discovered over two hundred eggs, which began hatching only moments ago," he said.

Colonel Hicks crossed to the bank of television screens. "If the military is listening, they must immediately destroy this building before they escape," he heard Nick say.

Suddenly the reporter shouted, "Oh, no, they're coming!"

Abruptly the camera swerved. Through the side window of the broadcast booth they saw dozens of crazed, yowling replicas of the great beast they had torpedoed.

"If those creatures escape and multiply," Nick was warning, "in a very short time this new species will replace us as the dominant creatures of this planet."

Colonel Hicks raced to the phone. "Code Dragonfly!" he shouted.

O'Neal scrambled to his feet. His men followed. The mayor rushed over to Hicks. "Isn't that the nerd you fired?" he demanded.

"You heard me," Hicks was saying into the phone. "I want you to blow up Madison Square Garden!"

He pushed past the mayor and rushed back to the TV monitors. The screen was filled with screeching, scrambling little monsters trying to break into the broadcast booth.

"What's happening now?" Hicks asked. "Where's Nick?"

Getting out of there fast, he hoped.

Phillipe had stayed out of camera range. Now that Animal's camera was focused on the raging mutants, he leaped into action.

Grabbing a spool of coaxial cable from a corner of the booth, the agent began tying it around a support beam. Nick ran to his aid.

"Regardless of what happens to us, this place must be destroyed before they can escape," Audrey was saying as the warring beasts hurled themselves against the glass. "Reporting live from Madison Square Garden, this is Audrey Timmonds, WIDF."

Animal lowered the camera. Everyone in the booth was silent.

Suddenly the computer began beeping. Animal lunged at it and read the incoming note.

"The good news is, they got the message," he told them. "The bad news is, we've got six minutes to get out of here."

Phillipe tugged at the fastened cable, then jumped to his feet.

"Okay, the party is over," he announced, spraying bullets into the front window and shattering it. As glass rained down, Phillipe tossed the cable out the broken window. "Anyone care to join me?"

Animal ripped one of the video cameras from its stand. Hoisting it to his shoulder, he rushed to the window. Phillipe slid down first, then covered Animal as he followed.

Audrey and Nick stared nervously at the long drop. The door behind them was beginning to give way. "Go," Nick urged.

She kissed him, then dropped from the booth.

The door behind Nick splintered. As the bellowing babies flooded into the room, he grabbed the cable and jumped.

With Phillipe firing at everything that moved, they raced into the main lobby.

At the top of the escalator, they froze. Below them, babies were tearing apart a concession stand, fighting over stale chocolate bars.

One by one the raging beasts stopped, sniffed the air, and looked up.

A large chandelier hung between them and the front

door. Phillipe fired a short burst, slicing the chain that supported it.

The fixture dropped and shattered. The creatures, startled, scattered.

Phillipe led the dash down the broken escalator.

They were a few feet from the doors when the babies charged again.

Nick grabbed a small candy machine and threw it back at the oncoming beasts. The glass globe broke. Thousands of gum balls rolled across the floor.

The shrieks became deafening as one after another the enraged babies slid, tumbled, and fell over the gum balls.

The sound of jet fighters filled the air above the Garden. "Go, go, go!" Phillipe urged as Nick, Audrey, and Animal dashed past him, out into the night.

With a final burst of gunfire, the Frenchman backed out, slid his rifle through the door handles, and ran.

The street rattled under the bombers. Missiles rained down. An enormous explosion erupted. Madison Square Garden, the most famous sports arena in New York, burst into towering flames.

Moments later, there was only silence.

13

The force of the blast had thrown Nick, Audrey, Animal, and Phillipe to the ground.

Nick sat up slowly. "Are you okay?" he asked Audrey.

She nodded. "I never thought your life was this exciting."

"You'd be surprised." He grinned.

Phillipe's cheek was bleeding, but he was all right.

As they got up, the street suddenly began to vibrate. The few bits of glass still trapped in windowpanes clattered fiercely.

A rumbling sounded underground.

It was followed by a ghastly wail.

Bursting up through the smoking remains of Madison Square Garden, the mammoth beast appeared.

"Godzilla!" Animal whispered. The submarines had not killed him after all.

Bleeding from his wounds, the mutant leaned down and nuzzled the burnt-out remains of his nest.

There was an awful expression on his face as he searched for his young. It was a look, Audrey thought, of terrible pain.

That pain turned quickly to burning rage. The huge head swung toward them, glaring.

"He looks angry," Nick whispered.

"So what do we do?" Animal asked.

"Run," Phillipe advised.

They darted down an alleyway as the furious beast pounced.

The towering creature charged after them, ripping buildings apart as he plowed through the alley.

Phillipe ran to a parked yellow cab. In one move, he drew a screwdriver out of his belt, popped the ignition device off the steering column, and hot-wired the car. It took less than fifteen seconds.

"Man, you're good," Animal said, holding the door open as Nick and Audrey piled in. With Animal barely inside, Phillipe hit the gas and took off.

The immense beast stepped into their path. The cab hit one of his huge toenails like a ramp and went airborne. It landed hard, skidding around the corner.

The enraged monster was right behind it. His huge jaws snapped at the car, but Phillipe gunned the motor, swerving just out of danger.

Animal filmed out the back window. "Better step on it, Frenchie!" he warned as the creature closed the gap between them.

With incredible skill and more than a little luck, Phillipe zigzagged through the city streets.

"Look out!" Audrey hollered as they crossed an intersection.

There was a wild screeching of brakes behind them.

Sergeant O'Neal's men had been speeding toward Madison Square Garden. "What was that?" O'Neal blurted, staring after the cab. The trucks behind him plowed into one another.

The street beneath them rumbled. O'Neal looked up.

"Godzilla!" a soldier yelled as a giant foot flattened a truck in its path.

O'Neal grabbed the radio off his belt. "Command, find Colonel Hicks," he called. "Godzilla is back!"

Nick looked back at the soldiers. "That was O'Neal," he said. "Turn around."

"Are you crazy?" Phillipe hollered.

"Do it!" Nick ordered, ripping the cab license off the dashboard.

As the beast ran toward them, Phillipe wheeled the cab around and the taxi roared through the massive legs.

O'Neal had reached Hicks. The colonel was ordering his F-18 bombers back into action.

O'Neal's men were trying to repair their trucks when the taxi returned, with the creature close behind it.

Leaning out of the speeding cab, Nick tossed out the taxi license.

O'Neal scrambled to pick it up. "Excellent," the sergeant muttered, impressed.

Minutes later, he was in a deserted taxi garage.

"What are we looking for, sir?" one of his soldiers asked.

"They keep a record of each cab's radio frequency," O'Neal said, flipping through a notebook. "Got it!" He slapped the page.

Across town, with the beast snapping at its rear bumper, the cab veered wildly onto Park Avenue.

"Nick, you there? Hello, come in, Worm Man." The cab's radio crackled to life.

"O'Neal!" Nick grabbed the radio as the taxi bounced onto a sidewalk and raced under the pedestrian walkway of a building site.

"Where are you?" the sergeant asked.

"Park Avenue South," Audrey told Nick as the creature crashed into a pyramid of construction pipes behind them.

"Nick, listen," O'Neal instructed. "Hicks has called in the airstrike. But you've gotta get Godzilla out into the open so we can get a clear shot at him."

"Where's the nearest suspension bridge?" Nick asked.

"Brooklyn," Audrey said.

"Which way?" Phillipe hollered.

"Downtown!" Audrey said.

Phillipe aimed the cab downtown, barreling through side streets, alleyways, underground garages, any place small and narrow enough to slow the mammoth monster.

"There!" Audrey shouted. The bridge was in sight. The cab sped up the on-ramp.

"I think we lost him." Animal looked out from behind his camera.

With an explosive blast, the on-ramp ripped open in front of them. The beast reared up.

Phillipe hit the brakes. The slippery road sent the taxi into a wild skid. It stopped underneath a big highway sign.

Jaws wide, the creature lunged to chomp down on the cab.

The steel sign above the car slammed into the roof of his mouth, preventing him from biting down.

Phillipe gunned the motor, but the cab's wheels spun helplessly against the gigantic tongue pushing at it.

The sign supports began to give way. An electric cable

came loose, dangling dangerously close to the car. Sparks shot from it.

Nick ripped off his jacket, wrapped it around his hand, and opened the door. Grabbing the cable with his wrapped hand, he jammed it into Godzilla's tongue.

There was an explosive burst of fire. Sparks crackled.

The shocked beast's mouth flew open. He pulled back his tongue. And the taxi's spinning wheels hit the road.

Landing hard on the pavement, the cab peeled out and zoomed onto the bridge.

The giant lizard wheeled around and followed it, the roadway heaving beneath him.

Phillipe slowed and swerved, then revved up again. It was like driving through an earthquake.

The great suspension cables that held the bridge stretched and contracted like rubber bands. The towers they threaded through began to sway.

As the beast crashed through the first set of towers, he got caught in the immense cables. The more he struggled, swatting at the big wires, the more entangled he became.

"He's stuck," Animal reported, trying to steady his camera.

Above the bridge, the air was suddenly filled with swooping F-18 fighter jets.

Phillipe raced through the second set of towering girders. They were almost across.

The massive creature screamed in frustration, fighting to free himself. The cables whipped against him, lashing his immense body again and again. Like a fly in an enormous web, he was frozen in the tangled wires.

The taxi got to the other side of the bridge and slid to

a stop. Nick and Audrey jumped out. Together they watched the desperate beast's terrible struggle.

A moment later the F-18s fired at the trapped reptile. Deadly missiles slammed into his chest, exploding. Bellowing in pain, the beast kept trying to free himself.

Audrey was crying. Nick wrapped his arms around her.

Again the bombers fired, the missiles screamed. The massive creature was hit again.

Animal kept filming. In back of him, behind the blockade, the mob that had gathered at the bridge watched in horror.

Mortally wounded, the immense beast reared up, screaming.

Audrey, Nick, and Phillipe moved back as the creature began to fall. Even Animal retreated.

Just as they stepped away, the enormous head came crashing down on top of the cab, crushing it completely.

The earth shook. Rocked by the impact, the crowd screamed. And then a stunned silence fell.

The creature's last breath escaped. Defeated and weary, his eyes blinked slowly as his life slipped away.

The shocked mob began to stir. There was a smattering of nervous applause, and then scattered shouts and cheering.

"Victor!" a joyful voice called. Animal set down his camera as Lucy burst from the crowd. He caught her in his arms and spun her around as she showered him with kisses.

They were mobbed by reporters.

"There's Tatopoulos," someone cried. "Dr. Tatopoulos, did Godzilla have a nest?" a reporter demanded. "Where did he come from?" another shouted. "Can you tell us what happened back there?"

Nick barely heard them. Even as he tried to comfort Audrey, he felt a strange and deep sadness at the sight of the toppled giant.

"Oh, no," Audrey whispered suddenly, moving out of his arms.

"Move it! Watch out! This is a WIDF exclusive, fellows!" Charles Caiman pushed to the front of the crowd.

"Who is that guy?" Nick asked.

"He's the one who stole my story — and your tape," Audrey said unhappily, even as she realized she wasn't entirely blameless.

The questions were coming fast and furiously. "Were you the first to see Godzilla? Where did he come from? Are there more of them? How did you track him down?"

"Sorry, guys." Nick grinned suddenly. "I've promised my story as an exclusive."

Caiman sprung from the crowd and ran to Audrey. "We did it!" he announced. "We've got the exclusive! Audrey, you're beautiful!"

"We did?" she said coldly. "I don't think so."

"Hey, remember, you work for me." Caiman's smile wavered.

"Not anymore, Chuck. I quit," she said.

"Audrey?" Animal was checking the pockets of his coat and jacket. "Did you take the tape out of the camera?" he called to her.

"Where's Phillipe?" Nick asked suddenly.

They looked around. He was gone, nowhere to be seen.

A phone began to ring. Nick patted his pocket and found Phillipe's cellular phone. He clicked it on.

"It's Phillipe," the familiar voice said. "Tell your friends I will send the tape after I remove a few items from it."

"Is it him?" Audrey mouthed. Nick nodded. "I understand," he told the French agent.

"Goodbye, my friend. Thank you for your help," Phillipe said.

"Wait," Nick urged. But the line went dead.

"Who was that Frenchman, anyway?" Audrey asked.

Nick looked at the lifeless beast the nuclear bomb tests had created, the "mistake" Phillipe had been sent to clean up. "Just some insurance guy," he said.

Afterword

Madison Square Garden was a mass of smoking wreckage. Weeks after the bombings, cleanup crews could still feel the heat.

Beneath the arena, Penn Station was also filled with smoldering rubble. Train tunnels had collapsed. Some would be shut for months. Others, lost under tons of collapsed steel, would never be used again.

In one such tunnel, far underground, protected by packed earth, a gigantic egg nestled.

As trains rumbled by on the few cleared tracks, the towering egg rocked slightly.

A crack formed in its shell.

It was a very small crack. It might have been made by the vibrations of the trains, or the jackhammers of the cleanup crews high overhead, or other forces outside the egg.

But it might also have come from within, from something inside the shell struggling to break free and live.